This Little Tiger book belongs to:

_____

_____

_____

_____

For Doris and George
~A. H. B.

For Matthew and Sally
~J. C.

LITTLE TIGER PRESS
1 The Coda Centre, 189 Munster Road, London SW6 6AW
www.littletiger.co.uk
First published in Great Britain 1996 as *What if?*
by Little Tiger Press, London
This edition published in 2013

Text copyright © A. H. Benjamin 1996
Illustrations copyright © Jane Chapman 1996

A. H. Benjamin and Jane Chapman have asserted their rights
to be identified as the author and illustrator of this work under
the Copyright, Designs and Patents Act, 1988

BAA! MOO!
WHAT WILL WE DO?

A.H. BENJAMIN and JANE CHAPMAN

LITTLE TIGER PRESS

Something special was happening on Buttercup Farm.
The farmer had bought a kangaroo, and it was arriving
that very day!

The farm animals had never seen a kangaroo before.

"What can a kangaroo do,
anyway?" they wondered.
But nobody knew.

"What if she can crow?" said Rooster. "What if she gets up very early every morning and crows so loudly that she wakes up the whole farm? Perhaps she would even count the hens and chicks to see if any are missing. Then the farmer wouldn't need me, and I'd have to look for another job. *Cock-a-doodle-doo!* I might not find one!"

"How dreadful!"

said everyone.

"What if she can herd sheep?" said Dog.
"What if she rounds them all up and takes
them to graze on the highest and greenest
hills? She might even chase a fox or two.
The farmer would be so pleased with her
that he'd send me to live in the kennels.
Woof! I would hate that!"

"How horrible!"

said everyone.

"What if she can catch mice?" said Cat. "What if she catches all the mice in the barn, and a few rats, too? Maybe even the spiders would be scared to live there. Then the farmer would get rid of me, and I would become a stray. *Meow!* I'd miss my milk and sardines!"

"What if she can give milk?" said Cow. "What if she fills up all the pails on the farm with such rich, creamy milk that everybody wants to buy it? Then nobody would want mine, and the farmer would make me pull the plow instead.
Moo! I'd miss my cozy stall!"

"How appalling!"

said everyone.

"What if she can grow wool?" said Sheep.
"What if she has a thick, woolly fleece that
is whiter than snow and softer than silk?
And maybe her coat will grow twice as
fast as mine. The farmer would be so
delighted that he'd only use *my* wool
to stuff old pillows and cushions.
Baa! I couldn't stand that!"

"What if she can pull a cart?" said Horse.
"What if she can take a cartful of fruit and
vegetables to the market faster than I can?
She might even give rides to the farmer's two
children. Then there would be no place for me,
and I would end up in an old horses' home.
Neigh! I'd miss all my friends here!"

"How frightful!"

said everyone.

They were so busy worrying that they
didn't notice that some of the young
farm animals were missing.

"Where are my puppies?" asked Dog.

"And my kittens?" asked Cat.
"And my lamb?" asked Sheep.

All the animals searched and searched, but they could not find them anywhere.

They looked from the barn . . .

. . . to the pigsty, with no luck.

"This is dreadful!" crowed Rooster.

"Horrible!" woofed Dog.

"Awful!" meowed Cat.

"Appalling!" mooed Cow.

"Terrible!" baaed Sheep.

"Frightful!" neighed Horse.

Suddenly, across the field they saw . . .

. . . a very strange animal,
leaping and bounding
toward them.

"Hello," it said.
"I'm Kangaroo!"

The animals couldn't believe
their eyes. Kangaroo had
a big pouch in her tummy,
and in the pouch . . .

. . . were
three kittens,
two puppies
and one
tiny lamb!

"We've had so much fun going on a tour of the farm," said Kangaroo. "What if I were to be their baby-sitter every day!"

"*What a good idea!*" the animals cried. And with crowing, barking, meowing, mooing, baaing, and neighing, they all welcomed Kangaroo to her new home.